# Little Red Riding Hood

Retold by Rebecca Heller
Illustrated by Marsha Winborn

A GOLDEN BOOK • NEW YORK
Western Publishing Company, Inc., Racine, Wisconsin 53404

Once there was a little girl who lived with her mother in a house at the edge of the forest.

The little girl always wore a red cloak and hood that her grandmother had made for her. That's why everyone, even her mother, called her Little Red Riding Hood.

One day Little Red Riding Hood's mother said to her, "Grandmother is not feeling well. I have packed a basket with fruit and cakes and honey. Will you take it to her?"

"Yes, Mother," said Little Red Riding Hood.

"Be careful going through the forest," said her
mother, "and don't dawdle along the way.
Grandmother is waiting for you."

"Yes, Mother," said Little Red Riding Hood, and
she took the basket and set out.

Little Red Riding Hood had gone but a short
way into the forest when a great gray wolf stepped
out from behind a tree.

"Good morning, Little Red Riding Hood," said
the wolf. "Where are you going on this fine day?"

"I am going to see Grandmother, on the other
side of the forest," said Little Red Riding Hood.
"She is ill, and I am bringing her fruit and cakes
and honey."

"Why not bring her some wild flowers as well?"
said the wolf. "There are so many to pick from here
in the forest."

"I cannot stop," said Little Red Riding Hood.
"Mother said I must not dawdle along the way."

"Picking flowers is not dawdling," said the wolf. "Besides, a bunch of pretty flowers will cheer your grandmother and make her feel better."

"Perhaps you are right," said Little Red Riding Hood. And she put down the basket and began to pick wild flowers.

Meanwhile, the wolf slipped away and sped to the other side of the forest. When he came to Grandmother's cottage, he crept up to the door and knocked.

"Who is it?" called Grandmother.

"It is I, Little Red Riding Hood," answered the wolf in a little high voice. "I have brought you fruit and cakes and honey."

"Come in, dear," said Grandmother. "The door is open."

As soon as the wolf was inside, he bounded over
to the bed and gobbled up Grandmother whole,
leaving only her shawl and nightcap.

He put on the nightcap and wrapped himself in
the shawl. Then he crawled into bed to wait for
Little Red Riding Hood.

Before long there was a knock at the door.
"Who is it?" called the wolf in a high little voice.
"It is I, Little Red Riding Hood," came the reply.
"I have brought you fruit and cakes and honey, and
a bunch of pretty wild flowers to cheer you."
"Come in," said the wolf. "The door is open."

Little Red Riding Hood went in and stood for a moment in the doorway. "Oh, Grandmother!" she said, looking over at the bed. "What big ears you have!"

"The better to hear you with, my dear," said the wolf. "Come closer."

"Oh, Grandmother!" said Little Red Riding Hood, stepping into the room. "What big eyes you have!"

"The better to see you with, my dear," said the wolf. "Come closer."

Little Red Riding Hood came closer. "Oh, Grandmother!" she exclaimed. "What big teeth you have!"

"The better to *eat* you with!" said the wolf, and he grabbed Little Red Riding Hood and gobbled her up whole.

Then, feeling full and satisfied, the wolf lay down and fell asleep.

Now it happened that a woodcutter was passing Grandmother's cottage just then. He knew the old woman had been feeling poorly, and he decided to look in on her.

When he saw the wolf snoring on the bed, he knew at once what had happened.

"I have you at last, you devil," he said, and he slew the wolf with his ax.

Then the woodcutter took a carving knife, and very carefully he slit open the wolf's belly. Out popped Little Red Riding Hood and her grandmother, safe and whole, just as the wolf had swallowed them.

"Oh, Grandmother!" cried Little Red Riding Hood. "How happy I am to see you!"

"And I am happy to see you, child," said Grandmother, giving Little Red Riding Hood a hug.

Then Little Red Riding Hood, Grandmother, and the woodcutter sat down to feast on fruit and cakes and honey. They all lived happily from that day on, never to be troubled by the wicked wolf again.